A Tune for Mule

by Liza Charlesworth

ISBN: 978-1-338-84443-6

Art Director: Tannaz Fassihi; Designer: Cynthia Ng; Illustrated by Michael Robertson
Copyright © Liza Charlesworth. All rights reserved. Published by Scholastic Inc.

3 4 5 6   68   26 25 24

Printed in Jiaxing, China. First printing, June 2022.

It is time to meet June.
It is time to meet Luke.

It is time to meet Mule.
Mule is cute AND magic!

June gave Mule a flute.
"Dute-a-lute-tute!" said Mule.

Mule made the flute HUGE!
Did June like it? Yes!

Luke gave Mule a sax.
"Dute-a-lute-tute!" said Mule.

Mule made the sax HUGE!
Did Luke like it? Yes!

June gave Mule a cube.
"Dute-a-lute-tute!" said Mule.

Mule made the cube HUGE!
Did June like it? Yes!

"I like the HUGE flute, HUGE sax, and HUGE cube," said Luke. "But how can kids use them?"

"I got it, dude!" said June.
"Mule, make me and Luke HUGE!"
"Dute-a-lute-tute!" said Mule.

Mule made June HUGE!
Mule made Luke HUGE!

Then June and Luke
made a HUGE tune for Mule.
Did Mule like it? Yes!

Read & Review

Invite your learner to point to each long-*u* word and read it aloud.

cube

Luke

flute

lute

14

huge

dude   June

tune

cute   dute   tute

mule   use

NOTE: *dute* and *tute* are nonsense words.

15

Fun Fill-Ins

Read the sentences aloud, inviting your learner to complete them using the long-*u* words in the box.

> dude Mule Luke huge tune

1. The kids in this story are June and

   _____.

2. They are friends with _____.

3. Mule can make things _____.

4. June said, "I got it, _____!"

5. They use a huge flute
   and sax to play a _____.